What Do Ducks Dream?

By HARRIET ZIEFERT

Illustrated by DONALD SAAF

G. P. Putnam's Sons   New York

On Sigmund's farm they all are sleeping;

Into night the dreams come creeping.

The cows all dream of heaps of hay

And fields of boats for floating away.

On seas as wide as they can be,

Horses dream of galloping free.

Fluffy ducks in their sleepy hours

Fly their bikes over hills and flowers.

Two pigs dream of pudding and pie

And reaching, reaching to the sky.

A rooster dreams of tomorrow's morn,

And waking neighbors with a giant horn.

White goats dream of hills so steep
And climbing trees for fruits to keep.

On Sigmund's farm they all are sleeping, but...

The barn owl, and the fox and snake,
These three are quite wide awake.

The fox thinks stealing chicks is nice;
The snake likes eggs; the owl hunts . . .

mice!

Inside the house on Sigmund's farm,
Everyone is safe from harm.

It is quiet; there's not a peep.
The children all are fast asleep.

From Anna, the baby, to the oldest, Mathilde,
With books and games their day was filled.

Now they're cozy in their beds.
What dreams have come inside their heads?

The children dream of making noise,

Of big, red berries and birthday toys.

The doggy dreams in his doggy head,
Of sleeping in little Martin's bed.

Kitty dreams in reds and blues,
Of dressing up in Mother's shoes.

A sweet dream is a wish from you.

If you're lucky, it may come true.

Good morning!

Author's Note

A little more than a hundred years ago Sigmund Freud's *The Interpretation of Dreams* was published.

In it Freud tells the story of his young daughter, Anna, who was not permitted to eat for a day because of an upset stomach. In her sleep that night Freud says she called out: "Anna Freud, stwawbewwies, wild stwawbewwies, omblet, pudden!" Freud interprets this as straight wish fulfillment: Anna went to sleep hungry; she dreamt of something to eat.

Freud says he does not know what animals dream of, but cites proverbs that suggest the dreams of animals may be pure wish fulfillment as well.

A Hungarian proverb declares, "Pigs dream of acorns and geese dream of maize." A Jewish proverb asks, "What do hens dream of?" And millet is the answer.

When an event surpasses expectations, we say with delight: "In my wildest dreams I never would have imagined such a thing." I am grateful to Sigmund Freud for leading me to imagine what ducks and other animals dream.

—Harriet M. Ziefert